Whose Baby?

Masayuki Yabuuchi

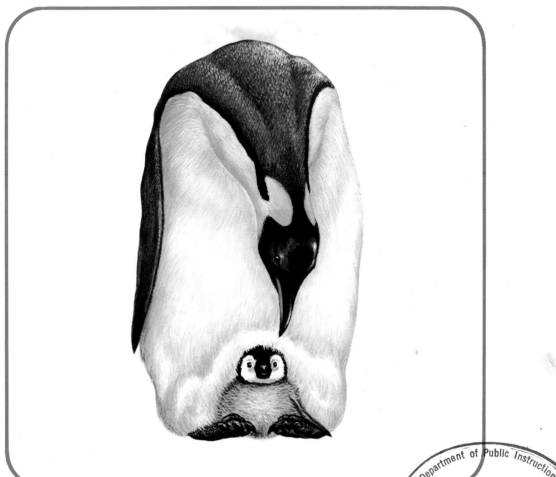

PHILOMEL BOOKS
New York

This is a fawn.
Whose baby is it?

A fawn is a baby deer.

It belongs to a mother and father deer,
called a buck and a doe.

Whose chick is this?

It belongs to a peacock
and peahen.

This cub is curled up fast asleep.
Whose baby is it?

It is a fox cub.

It belongs to a fox and a vixen.

This cub is wide awake —
whose cub is it?

It belongs to a lion and lioness.

This is a pup —
whose pup is it?

It belongs to a bull seal and a cow seal.

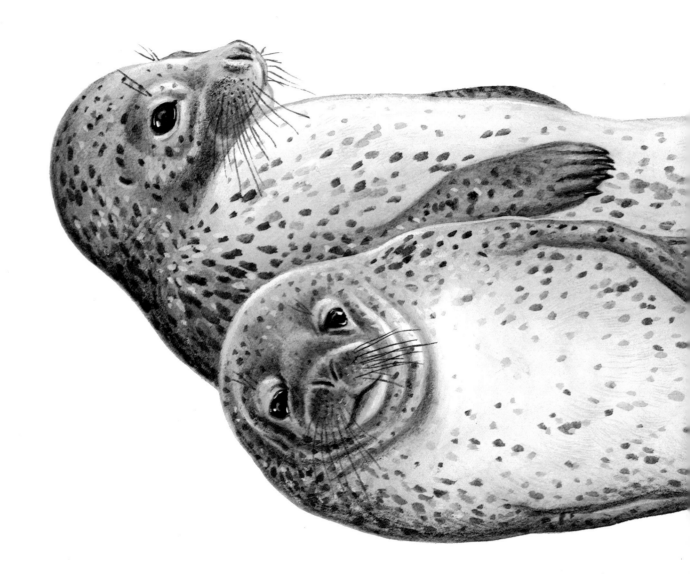

This is a calf.
Whose baby is it?

It is a baby bison.
It belongs to a bull bison
and cow bison.